10639195

NO FLEAS, PLEASE!

Written by Michael J. Pellowski
Illustrated by John Jones

Troll Associates

Library of Congress Cataloging in Publication Data

Pellowski, Michael
No fleas, please!

Summary: All of the animals try to get rid of the flea when it lands on them.
[1. Fleas—Fiction. 2. Animals—Fiction]
I. Jones, John, 1935- ill. II. Title.
PZ7.P3656No 1986 [E] 85-14066
ISBN 0-8167-0608-5 (lib. bdg.)
ISBN 0-8167-0609-3 (pbk.)

Copyright © 1986 by Troll Associates, Mahwah, New Jersey
All rights reserved. No part of this book may be used or reproduced in any manner whatsoever without written permission from the publisher.
Printed in the United States of America

10 9 8 7 6 5 4 3 2 1

NO FLEAS, PLEASE!

Boing! What is that sound? Boing! Boing! It is the sound of a flea jumping. Boing! Boing! Boing!

A flea was jumping through the woods. He jumped by a big lake. He jumped by big trees. What was that silly flea doing?

The flea was looking for a place to live.

Where is a good place for a flea to live? A lake is not a good place. A tree is not a good place. A good place is on an animal.

Fleas like to live on animals. But animals do not like fleas. Fleas make animals itch. Fleas make animals scratch.

Boing! Boing! The flea jumped and jumped. He looked and looked for an animal to live on.

Big Bear was an animal. He lived in the woods. The flea saw Big Bear.
"There is a good place to live," thought the flea. Boing!

"What was that sound?" said Big Bear.
He could not see the flea. But he could feel the flea. What a bad feeling it was!

"Oh no," cried Big Bear, "not a flea! Please, not a flea!"
But a flea it was. And Big Bear began to feel itchy. Poor, itchy Big Bear!

Big Bear scratched. He scratched the itch. He scratched here, there, and everywhere. Big Bear scratched at the flea. But the itching did not stop.

"This flea must go," yelled Big Bear. "I must find a better way to scratch!"

Big Bear had a scratching tree. Bears like to scratch their backs on trees. Big Bear's tree was by the lake. He went to scratch his big itch.

"Now I will make this flea go away," said Big Bear.
He scratched his back on the tree. Up he went. Down he went. Up and down he went scratching, scratching, scratching.

Nosey Otter was in the lake. He saw Big Bear. Otters are very nosey.

"What is that silly bear doing?" said the otter. "I will go and see."

Nosey Otter went up to Big Bear.
"Why are you scratching?"
Nosey Otter asked.
"I have a big itch," said Big
Bear. "A flea is on me."

"A flea," yelled the otter. "No fleas, please!"

Poor Nosey Otter. Being too nosey was bad for him. The flea saw the otter.

"A bear is not a good place to live," thought the flea. "Bears scratch too much. An otter is a better place to live."

Boing! What a sound! What a happy sound for Big Bear. What an unhappy sound for Nosey Otter.

"I feel better," said Big Bear.
"I do not feel itchy anymore."
Instead Nosey Otter felt an itch.
He had the flea.

Big Bear went away. Nosey Otter scratched and scratched. Oh, what a bad feeling! Poor, poor, itchy Otter.

"This flea must go," cried Nosey Otter.
Down to the lake went the otter. Into the lake he jumped.
The flea held his nose.

Up and down went Nosey Otter in the lake. He came out. He did not feel better. The itching did not stop. Nosey Otter scratched and scratched.

Raccoon was by the lake.
Raccoons like to live by lakes.
He saw Nosey Otter scratching.
Up to Nosey Otter went
Raccoon.
"You look silly," he said.

"I am not silly," said Nosey Otter. "I am itchy. A flea is on me." "A flea," cried Raccoon. "No fleas, please!"

The flea saw Raccoon.
"An otter is not a good place to live," thought the flea. "Otters go in lakes. I do not like lakes. A raccoon is a better place to live."

Boing! Nosey Otter stopped scratching—what a happy feeling! Raccoon began to itch—what an unhappy feeling! Poor, itchy Raccoon!

Into the lake jumped Nosey Otter. Away he went. Through the woods went Raccoon. Scratch! Scratch! Scratch!

"A flea! Why me?" cried Raccoon. "This flea must go. This itching must stop!"

Up a tree went Raccoon.
Raccoons like to go up in trees.
Up, up, up he went. He
scratched and scratched and
scratched.

In the tree was Busy Squirrel.
He was going down the tree.
Busy Squirrel saw Raccoon
scratching. He stopped being
busy.
"What are you doing?" he said.

"I have an itch," said Raccoon.
"I am scratching."

Raccoon's flea had a bad feeling. It did not like being up, up, up a tree.
"A raccoon is not a good place to live," thought the flea. "A squirrel is a better place. This squirrel is going down the tree."

Boing! Raccoon felt better. The itch was gone.
"What was that sound?" said the squirrel.
Raccoon cried, "It was the flea!"

"A flea," yelled Busy Squirrel.
"No fleas, please!"
Down the tree went Busy
Squirrel. Down went the flea.

Busy Squirrel began to itch. But he was too busy to scratch. Back up the tree he went. Down the tree he went. Up! Down! Up and down—what a busy, busy squirrel.

Busy Squirrel stopped.
"This flea must go," said Squirrel. "I cannot be busy and itchy, too."
He began to scratch and scratch.

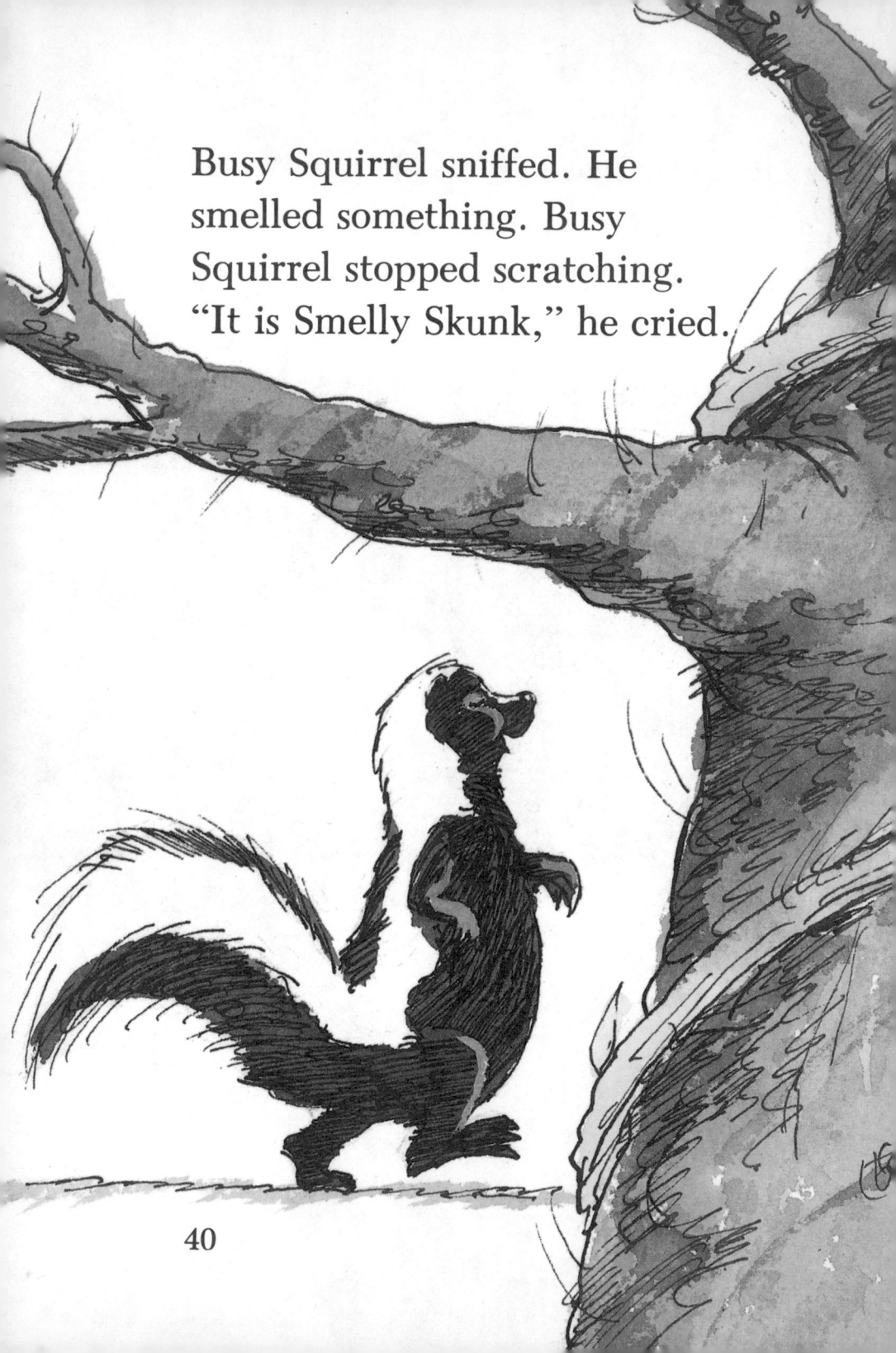

Busy Squirrel sniffed. He smelled something. Busy Squirrel stopped scratching. "It is Smelly Skunk," he cried.

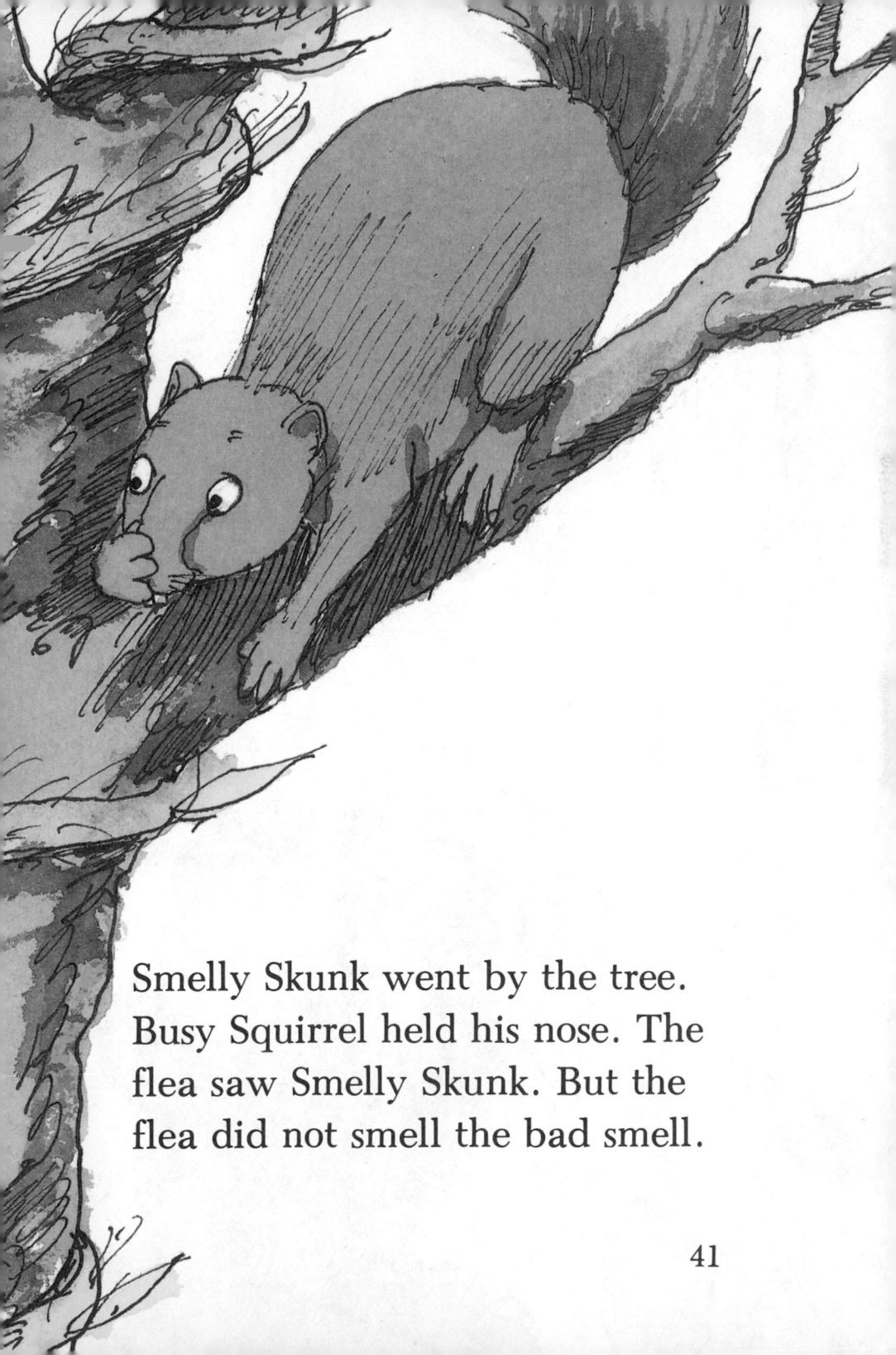

Smelly Skunk went by the tree. Busy Squirrel held his nose. The flea saw Smelly Skunk. But the flea did not smell the bad smell.

"A squirrel is not a good place to live," thought the flea. "A squirrel is too busy. There is an animal. That animal is a better place to live."

Boing! What a happy sound for Busy Squirrel. The itching stopped. Up the tree he went.

Smelly Skunk stopped. He began to feel itchy. He scratched and scratched. Poor Smelly Skunk.

The poor flea—*now* he smelled the skunk. What a bad smell! It smelled here. It smelled there. It smelled everywhere!

"This animal is not a good place to live," thought the flea. "This animal has a bad smell!"
Boing! Off the skunk jumped the flea.

Boing! Boing! Boing! Through the woods the flea jumped. He was looking for a place to live. A bear was not a good place. An otter was not a good place. A raccoon was not a good place. A squirrel was not a good place. And a skunk was not a good place.

Where is a good place for a flea to live? Not by me! No fleas, please!